Sorry Sam

ISBN 0-7696-4186-5

50395

EAN

9 780769 641867

S0-AUT-043

School Specialty®
Publishing

Text Copyright © Evans Brothers Ltd. 2005. Illustration Copyright ©
Evans Brothers Ltd. 2005. First published by Evans Brothers Limited, 2A
Portman Mansions, Chiltern Street, London W1U 6NR, United
Kingdom. This edition published under license from Zero to Ten
Limited. All rights reserved. Printed in China. This edition published in
2005 by Gingham Dog Press, an imprint of School Specialty Publishing,
a member of the School Specialty Family.

Library of Congress-in-Publication Data is on file with the publisher.

Send all inquiries to:
School Specialty Publishing
8720 Orion Place
Columbus, OH 43240-2111

ISBN 0-7696-4186-5

1 2 3 4 5 6 7 8 9 10 EVN 10 09 08 07 06 05

Sorry Sam

By Nick Turpin

Illustrated by Barbara Nascimbeni

GINGHAM DOG
PRESS

Columbus, Ohio

Sam ran outside.

Slam!

6

8

"Don't slam the door,"
said Mom.

10

"Sorry!" said Sam.

11

Splash!

14

Don't track in mud,"
said Mom.

15

"Sorry!" said Sam.

16

Hop!

"Don't jump on the bed,"
said Mom.

"Sorry!" said Sam.

It's bath time!

Squirt!

"Watch my eyes!"
said Sam.

"Sorry!" said Mom.

Words I Know

splash	jump
track	bath
ran	sorry
said	eyes

Think About It!

1. What did Sam do to the door?
2. What happened to the kitchen floor?
3. What did Sam jump on?
4. Why did Mom say she was sorry?
5. What makes this story funny?

The Story and You

1. Have you ever said "I'm sorry" and didn't really mean it? Tell about such a time.
2. Has someone ever said "I'm sorry" to you without really meaning it? How did it make you feel?
3. Why is it important to mean what you say?